I Am Winchell...

A Short Story by
Dick Wellman

*Dedicated to the memory of
my uncle Elton Ellsworth Wellman who lived much of this story.
He was in Johnson County, Wyoming during the Johnson County Cattle Wars
and is buried in Kaycee, Wyoming under the alias Albert W. Williams.*

1870-1960

I Am WhiteElk
Copyright © 2008 Marshall Publishing
P.O. Box 97
Sterling, KS 67579-0097

All rights reserved. No part of this publication may be reproduced in any form or by any means without the prior written permission of the publisher.

ISBN-13: 978-0-9745343-1-2
ISBN-10: 0-9745343-1-5

Library of Congress Control Number: 2008931431

Printed in the United States of America
by Mennonite Press, Inc., Newton KS 67114

Chapter 1

The first hint that today might be monumentally different than other days was the appearance of a pall of dust to the south on this hot windless day. The young brothers speculated as to its source and kept an eye on it from time to time when after midday the lowing of cattle could be heard.

"That just has to be a trail herd", reasoned Elt, the sixteen year old boy.

"But they are way east of the new Dead Line. They could be in for a lot of trouble!" exclaimed Ed, only twelve years old.

"That's a fact!" agreed Elt.

The Dead Line was a line established by the Kansas Legislature and was continually being moved west to keep the trail herds west of the wave of settlers establishing their claims. The line had just been shifted from Raymond, Kansas, just north of where the lads were herding cattle, to Dodge City, a hundred miles to the west. The reasoning for this line was supposedly to keep the trail herds from infecting the farmers' cattle with "Texas Fever." In reality, it was to keep the trail herds from trampling the crops of these new homesteaders. The Dead Line was enforced by lawmen and barbed wire fences, and Civil War veterans protecting their homes with rifles and marksmanship dearly learned. The veterans were given first choice as these lands were opened for homesteading.

How these two youngsters happened to be herding cattle out on this vast unfenced prairie was a story all its own.

The family: Father, mother and the two young boys, had left western New York state under a cloud of financial difficulties. They traveled west by train with two oxen, a driving team, wagon, plow, household furniture and, most incongruously, a sleigh used to travel the snow-covered roads and fields of rural New York. When they arrived in central Kansas, the sight of the sleigh brought looks of disbelief and laughter and outright scorn from the earlier immigrants to this arid land.

Monies for this trip and for the down payment on 160 acres of railroad lands near the town of Kansas Center had been provided by the family patriarch who, in return for the embarrassment brought on by his son's financial problems, disinherited him — even though the son eventually made good on all of his past obligations.

In order to get railroads built into the new territories, by an act of Congress in 1820, the Government gave the railroad companies every other section (640 acres) of land for 10 miles each side of the proposed line. The investment companies would then sell those properties to raise money to finance building of the railroads. They advertised and sent agents into the eastern states and to Europe to sing the praises of this promising land, and to invite the populace to share in this great opportunity.

But this family's "grub stake" was only sufficient for the first year. And when the rains refused to fall, as so often happens in this state, the meager crops that were growing fell victim to the grasshoppers and all was lost.

Reduced to renting a house in Peace, Kansas, Mr. Martin went to work on the Santa Fe and Topeka Railroad as a carpenter, building depots along the westward growth of the line abuilding.

Refusing to raise her sons in this wicked city of Peace, it was Jane who took her place as matriarch of the family. She took up a homestead in the "uninhabitable sand dunes" south of the Arkansas River.

Originally the family had looked to the cheap lands in Kansas as their "second chance." Now, with Jane in control, they vowed to establish a new life with this "third chance" on free lands. The homestead was 160 acres: sufficient for most of the homesteaders to starve on and sell out. Ultimately over 270 million acres of these "free lands" would be "taken up" by homesteaders.

From April through October, her young boys would herd cattle on the great unfenced prairie to the west of their home. The cattle were gathered from farmers, north of the river on the "hard ground," who paid to have them cared for during the farming season.

The boys established a cow camp some 10 miles west of the homestead on Dead Horse Creek.

According to Ed's diary, "We built a lean-to with willow sapplings (sic) and built us a coreal (corral) for the horse and donkey."

Each boy would take his turn herding the cattle for four days at a time while his brother helped at home with the farm work. Then the other brother, with a four-day supply of grub, would ride out to relieve his brother who would return to the farm to help his Ma.

Although neighbors would scoff at Ed riding a donkey, he realized that his donkey with its leisurely gait and calm demeanor had a gentling effect on the cattle.

The boys became sharpshooters at an early age, and prairie chicken and rabbit became staples in the family diet.

Elt even supplied ducks and geese he had shot to the grocer in town in exchange for such staples as flour, sugar, beans and dried fruit. Attendance in the one-room Triumph school was pretty haphazard and allowed him a lot of time to hunt. The economic need to make every shot count contributed to making this boy a renowned marksman.

On a return trip from town one evening, Elt came upon an old Indian man, just south of the river nearly frozen to death. Elt tied him across the saddle and led his horse and its burden home in the gathering night.

The old man, along with three young braves, were only one of many groups that slipped away from Darlington Reservation in Indian Territory. The old man had counseled against leaving Darlington with Chief Dull Knife the previous year, reasoning that things would get better. But when they didn't, he agreed to leave with the three youngsters. He ordered them to abandon him when he became ill and could not keep up with them in their flight.

This happened within a year of Chief Dull Knife's escape from Darlington with more than three hundred of his people. They headed north towards their former home. Dull Knife was actually better known among the Cheyenne as "Morning Star".

The same conditions that led Dull Knife and his band to leave the reservation still existed at Darlington. The promised annuities and the medicines and food were still not being provided. The lack of bison meat could be explained by the vanishing numbers of buffalo out on the plains, unceremoniously slaughtered for their hides or even just their tongues. The Indians resented attempts to substitute beef for their promised bison meat.

The several "hot-head" young braves in the entourage of Chief Dull Knife left nearly one hundred dead white men along their northward trail and knowledge of those atrocities was still fresh in the minds of the homesteaders.

(As a matter of historical fact, in 1879, Indians from the Territory escaped and tried to make their way back north to their homelands. The county paper stated that Sheriff Wm Smith issued this alarm: "Indians on the war-

path. Headed north. Liable to reach Lyons almost anytime. Get your guns in readiness and bring them to the courthouse at 2 o'clock. Don't fail if you want to protect your loved ones!"

To this report, Ed's diary added the following insight: "This band of Indians stopped at our place and slept in our barn. Wanted to eat our dog. We fed them pancakes for supper and breakfast. A real scare for us!")

"Dear Lord, what have you done?" queried a very frightened Jane when Elt, with Ed's help, carried the near lifeless old man into the warmth of the family's shanty.

Warmth was merely relative in this homestead shanty of board and batten construction with no interior walls. True, in out of the wind, it was warmer than outside in the great out-of-doors. The main fuel was bundled grass, soaked in the ever present tub of water so that it would not burn too fast in a custom stove designed just for this fuel. In the severest of weather, ear corn might be burned since it was cheaper than coal. It took hard cash to buy coal at the lumber yards in town. Hard cash was very difficult for many families to come up with.

As for burning wood, there was a total lack of trees in this area, even along the banks of the nearby Arkansas River. Grass fires, mostly started by lightning, swept the prairie clear of old grass accumulations and of saplings. The Indians had long before associated prairie fires with a renewing of lush grass as a lure for the buffalo in the early spring. They often purposely set fires to ensure a quick regrowth of grass. In some instances, Indian set fires to deny the travelers along the nearby Santa Fe Trail grazing for their livestock in the late dry summers.

Before construction of the shanty was begun, a 20-foot-wide fireguard had been plowed around the building site to protect it from fire. The sight or smell of smoke in the air struck near panic in those early day settlers; brigades of neighbors with wagons loaded with barrels of water and burlap sacks to be soaked and used to beat out the flames would converge on any fire. Neighbors were truly dependent upon one another.

Jane's fear that this uninvited "hostile" might murder them in their sleep was a genuine fear. A shotgun was kept just inside the door and was shown to every stranger that might be announced by the barking of the family dog.

"But Ma, he was going to freeze to death out there," pleaded Elt. "I couldn't leave him. And if you believe in what the Bible tells us as we read it every night … he is one of God's children, too ….Surely I done right."

Jane was pleased that the reading of the Bible had somehow reached this restless and growing young man. It was a great reward to her, so she relented in her opposition to this Good Samaritan act of her son.

"All right," she said reluctantly. "We will try to nurse him back to health, but we really should turn him over to the sheriff. And if any of our neighbors who have lost family to the Indians find out, they are liable to drag him out and kill him right before our eyes. We must tell no one!"

After only a few days in the shanty, the Indian was ensconced in a remote corner of the barn. Insulated by hay and wrapped in buffalo robes and fed warm soups and stews by Elt, he continued to recover.

Elt and the grateful Indian spent many hours smiling at one another and trying to converse by signing and laughing a lot.

In the days of his recovery, the old man would use his limited knowledge of "Reservation English" to converse with Elt, and the two supplemented this with their own devised sign language. Elt demonstrated that he was an adept student at learning the basic Cheyenne language.

One of their first exchanges was when the old man pointed to his chest and said, "Me, Old Running Horse," and, pointing to Elt, asked, "You?"

"Elt." was the straightforward reply.

The old man broke into laughter. He heard Elt to say "Elk" — food from the Big Horn Mountains of home.

Between tears of laughter, Old Running Horse said, "I think you better be WhiteElk!"

And so blossomed a great friendship.

As strength began to return, it was evident from his bearing that Old Running Horse was a man of authority and prestige within his tribe.

Elt skipped more school and stepped up his hunting. He took more and more geese and ducks to the grocer in return for the additional groceries they needed. This did not escape the notice of the grocer who asked if they had additional family now.

A flustered and uneasy Elt replied, "No, just friends on their way West," an obvious lie for this season of the year.

On one occasion, Old Running Horse showed Elt a scar on his chest from an arrow wound many years ago. Elt then revealed a long white scar on his right forearm, left there when he had carelessly fallen out of the hay mow and near impaled himself on a spike.

Such an innocent revelation would one day save his life.

Then, one evening in early spring when Elt returned from a trip to town for groceries, he discovered Old Running Horse was missing.

Elton and Old Running Horse Sign   *Illustration by David Cook*

A desperate and distraught boy made plans to track the old man down, but his mother, wise Jane, convinced Elt, "You have done what the Lord would have you do — and now it is time for the old man to do what he feels he has to do. You need to leave it at that, and respect him for what he obviously thinks he must do.

"And Elton," she added, "I want you to know that I have never been more proud of you than I am right now. I feel you have helped make me a better Christian by your example, and I thank you."

The following winter, the Blizzard of '86 reduced the cattle herds of the high plains by millions of heads and bankrupted many a cattle outfit, big and small. It also hit the tiny holdings of the Martins.

"The storm raged for three days," Ed wrote in his diary. "The first day we didn't even venture out of the house. The second day, we tied hay in our lariats to take to the cattle but the second we stepped out of the shelter of the barn the hay was gone."

The moist breath of the cattle froze on their muzzles and had to be broken off before the critter could eat!

"We didn't lose any cattle during the storm," Ed's diary continued, "but many in the spring were lost when we were out of feed and could not buy any."

The revulsion of having to helplessly watch cattle starve was too much for Elt and he secretly promised himself he would leave this harsh and unforgiving land the very first chance he had.

The pall of dust and the lowing of cattle was to be the answer to his resolve, although it was not apparent at the moment.

Just that morning, Ed had arrived to take Elt's place as herder, but Elt decided early on to stick around until the dust pall mystery was solved.

When they realized a trail herd was involved, Elt said, "Quick! Let's drift our cattle east towards home, and then come back over here and give them a look-see."

The unmistakable, ramrod straight military bearing of Colonel Rice, late of the Confederate Cavalry, drew the boys instinctively to his side. And as they were trading "Howdys," a rider galloped in from the north — the coarse and belligerent scout, Slayton.

With a mock salute, Slayton, a trailwise rider, announced, "Colonel, the biggest body of water we've seen since we left Texas is just three or four miles beyond the yonder ridge of hills. A great place to water and rest the night!"

"Begging your pardon Mr. Colonel," Elton broke in. "But that is a salt marsh, and if these thirsty cattle reach it you might lose them all!"

"Whoever heard of a salt marsh in the middle of Kansas?" sneered the disbelieving Slayton.

"Well, the Indians have been coming here for a thousand years to collect salt from the evaporative ponds, and now even white men come from the east to gather it," was Elt's response.

"If that is saltwater ahead, where the hell can we get fresh water?" demanded Colonel Rice. The Colonel was addressing Elt, not Slayton.

Elton and Ed Meet Col. Rice   *Illustration by David Cook*

   "Mr. Colonel, there are artesian springs about eight miles west of here, but if I was you, I'd circle back south a ways. If these thirsty critters see that marsh or smell that water, I'll bet they'd be hard to hold. And that's a fact. I'd be glad to lead you to them springs if you'd like, sir."

   Slayton warned,"Colonel that'd be way outta our way to the Raymond crossing — we could go east a-ways and not lose so much time."

   "Beggin yer pardon agin, Mr. Colonel, but due north of them springs is a solid bottom ford on the Arkansas, right near where Ft. Zarah used to be. It's much safer, and I know you'd really not be welcome near Raymond since the Dead Line has been moved west clear to Dodge City."

"Slayton, turn this herd back to the south right now," ordered the Colonel.

"Sonny, I'd be glad to pay you to lead us to the springs. Won't you please take the point?"

A sour Slayton did as he was ordered, but Elt realized he had made an enemy.

"Ed," Elt instructed, "keep our cattle drifted to the east and I'll be back in the morning. Then I'll go back to the farm."

"But, Elt! Ma is expecting you this afternoon. She'll be worried to death if you don't show up."

"I'll explain it to her tomorrow; don't worry yerself none. I'll be back tomorrow morning."

"Promise?"

"'Course I promise."

And then a proud, barefoot boy on an unshod spotted pony and rough saddle took his place at the point of a cattle herd, if for only for a few miles. He was in his glory and reasoned that this was to be his destiny.

The purity of the artesian water and the abundance of the lush grasses it watered provided the best overnight they'd encountered on the entire drive. The Colonel wisely decided to hold up for an extra day and rest the cattle, horses, and the drovers.

Colonel Rice recognized the inherent frontier savvy of this youngster and after much thought offered to take him on at man's pay if he'd join the drive.

An exuberant Elt was flattered by the offer of so much money, and recognized it as that opportunity to leave this hostile land that he'd been praying for. He all but rejoiced, except for thoughts of his brother Ed, who worshipped him, and Ma who loved, respected and really depended on him.

Ma most of all.

Next day Elt returned to the cow camp on Dead Horse Creek. He was astride a horse from the drive's remuda, leading his paint pony with its rough and wretched saddle and bridle.

Ed instinctively read the signs correctly and blurted out, "Elt, you can't go with them. Ma needs us both at the farm."

With real misgivings, Elt handed the reins of his paint pony to Ed and said, "Take care of Little Spot for me." Then he got off of his horse and hugged his younger brother, who turned away with tears in his eyes. As a shudder wracked his body, he heard Elt say, "Tell Ma that I'll be back."

Chapter 2

The first day's drive north from the artesian wells was uneventful and the beeves with their gorged bellies took to it readily. The lead steers took up their positions, and before nightfall they had reached the firm bottom crossing on the Arkansas near Old Fort Zarah and they crossed to the northern river bank to bed down. Colonel Rice became well aware of the great value this farm boy brought to the venture.

The Arkansas River at this point was usually "a hundred yards wide and six inches deep," with spots of treacherous unpredictable quicksand that seemed to shift location from day to day. But a cloudburst high in the Rockies, 500 miles away, might send a wall of water coursing down the channel sweeping everything before it. Even a sudden rain in one of the nearby tributaries could raise havoc. Herds were usually crossed over the water courses before nightfall for the fear that a rising stream might prevent a crossing the next morning. Routinely, "Cookie" pointed the wagon tongue towards the North Star; in case it was foggy or overcast the next morning, they would know in which direction to head.

Nothing remained where Ft. Zarah had been, but there was a "trading ranch" nearby which featured hardware, groceries, and mules for sale. The dugouts from an earlier encampment had caved in, and grasses were starting to heal the wounds to this land. The colonel took Elt to the store and bought for him a pair of used, proper leather boots along with appropriate clothing for the harsh conditions he would be facing. One drover had left the drive at Ft. Reno in the Cherokee Outlet, and his canvas suggans became a combination bedroll and suitcase for Elt.

And soon the routine of the drive gave Elt the opportunity to know the other drovers:

Colonel Amos Rice, late of the Confederate Cavalry. An authoritative man whose penetrating eyes seemed to take in everything in detail. His plantation had been ravaged during Sherman's "March to the Sea" and then was appropriated by Yankee carpetbaggers.

"Cookie" Augmon, a freed slave, who was totally devoted to "Massah Amos." "Cookie" drove the chuck wagon/bed wagon and would prepare hot foods day or night for the drovers.

Patrick O'Rourke. His aristocratic Irish father had spirited Patrick off to the New World rather than have him marry Edith, the voluptuous daughter of their housekeeper. Edith was great with his child. Once in the New World, Patrick found himself disinherited and with few funds. He vowed to one day return to Ireland and claim Edith and their child as his family, a goal he would never achieve.

Peter O'Toole. Another Irish lad from the boroughs of New York City. He had run away from home at an early age to escape the beatings of his step-father. He vowed to one day avenge those beatings and rescue his mother from that relationship. Initially, he was suspicious of the aristocratic O'Rourke, but they became fast friends as days on the trail proved their dependence upon one another.

Mark Slayton. Bloodthirsty when the odds were in his favor. A deserter from the Union army during the battle at Bull Run, he assumed this new name and fled ever southward and westward to escape his real identity. He resented a Confederate officer being the trail boss.

"Dusty" Rhodes had served as a sergeant under the Colonel and swore to follow him to the ends of the earth.

"Wild Bill" Jones. Son of a Missouri sharecropper, he wearied of clearing forests for a bit of farmland. He joined one of the last of the Santa Fe Trail caravans and then just drifted down to West Texas.

Anthony Rodriguez was an orphan who was just drifting around south Texas when he joined the drive. He came to look upon Colonel Rice as a father figure.

Casper Smith, a drifter. He would always be without a goal or an inspiration.

Tommy Aikens was the "horse jingler," and he had a much better rapport with the horses of the remuda than he did with the other drovers.

Cecil Thomas. Secretive. A loner and a very competent horseman. He was not given to conversation or to smiling. The last day of the drive, the other drovers would be no closer to him than they had been the first day of the drive.

"Cookie" was impressed that Elt always cleaned his tin plate before putting it into the "wreck bucket" where all of the utensils would eventually be scalded. Elt sensed the friendship offered by the combination cook and wagon driver. In the case of this small drive a single wagon served as both chuck wagon and bed wagon to haul the suggans.

Early on, Elt was assigned night hawk duties to circle the bedded down herd at a distance, usually humming or singing some ditty so as to not suddenly come upon a critter and scare it. Elt was cautioned that in lighting a cigarette, always ride at least a hundred yards away from the herd before striking a match, and to be sure to shield the light with cupped hands while turning away from the herd. The scratching of a match had been blamed for starting many a stampede, but this caution was not needed for this idealistic Baptist boy. Tobacco had been a stranger to his family.

This small herd of 2,260 head of 4-year-old steers was headed for the Rosebud and Pine Ridge Indian Agencies in South Dakota. Six hundred head to each of the agencies under a government contract. The remainder would be skirted south of the Black Hills and then north to Miles City, Montana to be sold. There were, in addition, sixty cows taken along to make the herd handle easier. There would be a ready market for them to help replenish the depleted herds of Montana.

Before Elt joined the drive, there were two riders in the lead, including the colonel; two riders in the swing and two riders in the drag; a horse wrangler who stayed behind with the extra horses, the cook and two extra cowboys. The drive was planned to make twelve to fifteen miles a day, depending on the water and the camp. This was a grazing drive, not an endurance run.

The cowboys rode all day, and every man had to stand a two hour night watch. They soon learned to sleep at a moment's notice.

The steers were all colors. Most were longhorns, but a few Hereford crosses were in the bunch. They were easy to handle if nothing happened to excite them.

When time permitted, Elt would help the horse "jingler" herd the horses of the remuda. Elt had always known the importance of hoof care for the horses, but his years in the sand hills had not prepared him to shoe horses. He had only trimmed the hooves of his family's ponies, draft horses and the team of oxen. He felt an obligation to help the jingler every chance he got, and soon became an excellent farrier in his own right.

The drovers rotated positions on the drive from time to time from point, to flank, to riding drag. Riding drag was the toughest job of them all. The drag rider's duty was to keep the weaker and slower cattle pushed up with the rest of the herd. In dry, still weather, the dust at the back of the herd would be almost intolerable. The "wild rag" neckerchief could filter a certain amount of dust from the rider's lungs when tied over their noses and mouths, but nothing could keep the dust from their eyes. Even worse was driving a herd into the wind which they instinctively resisted.

Somewhere in the rolling hills just south of the Platte, a wild-eyed and bloodthirsty Slayton, in a headlong gallop, approached the herd from the north shouting, "Colonel! There are Indians ahead in our path! Just a small band that we can wipe out easily!"

Elt, who had entertained the drovers with his knowledge of Cheyenne speak and sign language, pleaded with Colonel Rice to be allowed to meet and powwow with the Indians.

The Colonel was impressed with the boy's apparent lack of fear, and quickly gave his permission, much to Slayton's undisguised resentment.

Stripped to his underwear and riding bareback and weaponless to indicate to the Indians that they had nothing to fear from him, Elt rode to meet them with an arm upraised in a salute of peace. And then he said, "I am WhiteElk, friend of Old Running Horse." The conference lasted only a few minutes before Elt returned.

"Colonel, sir! They are no threat to us. There are only a few families. No warriors among them. They are off hunting buffalo. There are just old people and women and children, and sir, they are starving. Their range has been burned along with their tipis and their food supplies. They had to jump into the river to escape the fire and their only possessions are on their backs. Sir! Them children are starving, honest!"

An angry Slayton interjected, "We don't have extra food to share with them heathens, Colonel!"

"But Colonel," replied Elt, "We have three straggler steers that will never make the rest of the journey and they slow us down every mile of the way. Let me cut them out and give them to those poor souls."

Colonel Rice, with a new appreciation for the young boy's talents and mighty relieved that a confrontation had been avoided, agreed to Elt's request and instructed that the stragglers be sorted off and given to the Indians.

Then, in a tone somewhere between derision and admiration, the Colonel addressed Elt: "Boy, I think you should have been a God-damned missionary!" And he secretly smiled to himself.

Elt had driven the wedge between himself and Slayton a little deeper. But the story of this good deed would be told around many campfires, and at a later date the good deed would be repaid.

"I am WhiteElk, Friend of Old Running Horse"   *Illustration by David Cook*

This dry summer meant there was little swimming water to cross on the Arkansas, the Smoky, the Platte or the Nirabrara, and it was easy to put the herd into the shallow waters to drink and push them on to the other shore.

The seasoned riders soon found a new respect for this boy they had once made fun of, and whose relationship with the colonel they initially had resented.

One still night, the air was so oppressive that the men had trouble trying to sleep. There was lightning in the far distance, much too far away for the thunder to be heard. Near midnight, the colonel ordered the watches to be doubled, and "Cookie" allowed, "I bet there's trouble abrewin'."

The first clue was a gentle rustling of the grasses, and soon a great roar as the wind gathered force. The cattle became restless and were getting to their feet, trying to determine what to do next.

"Every man to his saddle!" shouted the colonel, just as the storm broke in all of its fury, in a great flash of lightning and crash of thunder, followed by almost continuous lightning strikes all across the horizon. Between moments in the jet black of night and the blinding flashes of lightning, the cattle could be seen milling in disarray and then breaking into a terrified, flat-out gallop ahead of the downpour and the hail.

Elt was soon aware that the hair on the back of his neck was standing on end. Sparks of electricity started jumping between the tips of the ears of his now fractious mount, and then balls of fire seemed to run down the pony's neck and in under the saddle. Sparks would jump from horn to horn on the terrified cattle. And then Elt noticed that a line of sparks were reaching for his pony's belly from his spurs. Correctly fearing that he might become attractive to a lightning strike, Elt reined in his horse, removed his spurs and placed them inside his leather saddle bag before continuing the chase.

He was later to learn that this phenomenon is referred to as "St. Elmo's Fire."

Tales of men and horses being trampled to death by stampeding herds always lingered just under the surface of every drover's consciousness. It was important to stay up with the herd, trying to haze them into circling from the flanks with yells and sometimes pistol fire.

It was more important to survive, and then when the cattle were "run out" to be ready to account for the cattle and gather them back into a trail herd once the storm had passed. At one point, Elt felt himself being surrounded by the thundering hooves as some had broken out from the flank

On the Drive to the Agencies *Illustration by David Cook*

and were running on each side of him. He instinctively started to work his way through them in the direction where the flank had once been. When the run was over, some six miles from its start, Elt gave way to a shuddering realization of what he had been through and praised the Lord for his safety with a fervor he had never known before.

Soon after daybreak he was able to catch a fresh horse from the remuda, saddle him, and turn his exhausted mount free to graze. It took the entire day to shepherd the cattle and horses back to the previous night's bed ground. Most of the riders had not eaten for nearly 24 hours, and in spite of the plenteous hot food provided for them, some were too tired to eat or to even speak. Only a few beeves were unaccounted for. A few had tumbled into gullies, and because of broken legs, had to be destroyed. The carcasses of only a couple could be salvaged for food, as they would surely spoil before they could be utilized. The horses gathered around the "bell mare" and were all accounted for.

The weather was overcast the next morning. "Cookie", as always, had pointed the wagon tongue towards the North Star and thus, it served as a compass to start the day's drive.

After a day's rest and then crossing the Smoky, the Platte and the Niobrara without having to swim the cattle, the herd was held in the sand hills of South Dakota.

The contract called for 300 steers to be delivered each week to the government corrals. Three riders — Elt, Dusty, and Cecil — would cut out the cattle pointed out to them by the Colonel to be delivered while the other six riders would stay and hold the herd.

At the Rosebud Agency, the cattle were delivered just at nightfall. The next morning at sunup, the country was full of Indians waiting for the beef to be "issued." Many were dressed in their finest, including war bonnets! It was the most spectacular scene that Elt had ever witnessed. The steers were then run through a chute and branded "RC" for received. They were then counted and run back through another corral, then through the chute again and branded "IDC" for Indian Department and Issued.

The steers were run out of the chute, one at a time, through a lane of Indians about twenty feet wide. The interpreter would call out an Indian's name and the Indian would follow the steer on horseback for about a hundred yards and then shoot him out on the open prairie. He would then drop off of his horse and he and his family would butcher the steer on the spot. After the three hundred head were run out and butchered, the flats for half a mile square were covered with Indian families in various stages of dressing their beeves! The families kept right on butchering when another Indian ran a steer by and dropped him!

When the big Blue-Roan steer that always seemed to be in the lead was run out, the trail riders looked on with misgivings. He had been the first to graze when they were turned out and the first back to the herd to trail on. The drovers thought the world of "Old Blue." Old Blue came out of the chute like a shot and ran for nearly two hundred yards before the Indian could catch up with him. The Indian laid right up alongside him and shot him through the "lights." Old Blue fell and rolled about four times and never kicked. There wasn't a dry eye among the drovers who hung their heads and averted each others eyes.

After the cattle had been delivered to both the Rosebud and Pine Ridge Agencies, the remaining herd was driven west, skirting the Black Hills, and then northward to Miles City, Montana and the Union Pacific railroad. The wide streets, which had been laid out with trail herds in mind, were nearly deserted as pedestrians sought the shade and protection of the raised store front walkways and awnings. Buggies were moved around the corners and the trail herd had the undisputed right of way. Even the painted ladies in the upstairs windows of the brothels showed bits of inviting flesh, but without the rowdy talk that would fill the saloons once the herd was corralled.

When the gates were finally closed on the shipping pens, then and only then did the switch engine give the least hiss as it started to do its work shunting the cattle cars to the load-out docks. Several of the drovers had never seen a steam locomotive before, but had heard tales of hearing the train whistles from miles off. But that sound would not be heard today.

Only weeks before, a thoughtless and impatient engineer had blown the train's whistle and that act cleared the stockyards as cattle took out most of the backyard fences and gardens in town. One of the enraged drovers rode up and took a shot at the engineer. Even though he missed the engineer, he did hit a glass sight gauge and the cab was filled with scalding steam. For months to come, any new train crew member was admonished, "You blow that whistle, and we could both wind up dead."

When the herd was settled for and the cowboys paid off, it was celebration time after the long months on the trail. The Colonel's warnings about the traps that might ensnare his crew fell on deaf ears. Baths, haircuts, new clothes, whiskey and female companionship were purchased with wild abandon. Elt only looked on with amusement while he planned for all of the things he would buy for Ma when he got home.

Dusty, "Wild Bill", and Tommy, the horse jingler, would ride the train with the colonel back to Chicago. The colonel, Dusty, and Tommy would be in Pecos the next spring to assemble another trail herd. But "Wild Bill" would return to the farm in Missouri, his wanderlust sated.

Slayton would die in a barroom fight without ever leaving Miles City, depriving him of his avowed pledge to "do in" that farm kid that he had so despised.

Cecil signed on with a local rancher and dreamed of the day he would own his own spread.

The Irish lads, Peter O'Toole and Patrick O'Rourke, heard of land still available for homesteading just east of Circle. They hoped to stake claims on adjacent homesteads and work them together. They rode off with great enthusiasm for their next adventure.

Casper was never seen again after he was paid off, and pointedly said goodbye to none of his compadres on the trail.

Anthony Rodriguez decided to stay in Miles City and work for the railroad.

"Cookie" would drive the chuck wagon back to Pecos for the next year's trail drive. Elt would ride with "Cookie" as far south as Dodge City where he planned to catch a train east to the village named Peace and to his family.

Chapter 3

There was a ready market for the trail-wise, well broke horses of the horse herd. The horse herd that had been known as "remuda" when it started out in Texas, became the "cavvy" somewheres in Wyoming and on up into Montana.

Three of the drovers headed for Chicago on the train, as did Colonel Rice, who would eventually catch another train to near the Pecos country before next year's drive. The drovers didn't necessarily have that same destination. Wild Bill would return to his home on a Midwest farm, his wanderlust sated. Others were headed wherever the trail might lead them. Several recognized the great grasslands of Montana as their promised land and would remain there to seek their fortunes, already seasoned cowboys.

The only elements backtracking the route of the drive would be "Cookie" with his horses and chuck wagon, a spare team, Elt and his chosen horse and the Colonel's favorite Morgan horse, Pride. Since there were fewer suggans and no need to carry extra water barrels on the familiar return route, the wagon was much lighter. And with no herd to set the pace, the return trip promised to take only one-half as long as the drive north.

Elt spent long hours lounging on the few suggans, while the extra horses tagged along. By the same token, he would drive the team while Cookie rested. Meals were prepared only twice a day, just before daylight and at the end of the day. Traveling the route in the opposite direction that they had originally taken would have made it seem unfamiliar if they hadn't been cautioned to always look back from time to time so as to be familiar with the terrain by looking at it from both directions.

Adding urgency to the trip was the evidence that fall was fast approaching and that bitter winter might not be far behind. The tall grasses were turning color and setting seed in the age-old race to procreate themselves. Even though the seeds were very nutritious, the stems were turning fibrous and unpalatable. But the short-grass buffalo and gamma grasses were meant for winter. As they matured, they were the nutritious feed that would lure the buffalo back south as winter approached. The early morning chill called for quick harnessing, early hot coffee and breakfast, and a return to the trail as soon as there was sufficient light.

Elt spent endless hours planning what he would buy to make life easier for Ma when he got home. The wages he had earned and had guarded so zealously were heavy in his pockets, and as each day brought them closer to Dodge City he became more and more impatient to get there. Once there, he could take the train back to Peace and a great homecoming with his family.

As they came over the last ridge that gave them a view of the Arkansas River Valley, they were impressed with the new city of Dodge, just upriver from Old Fort Dodge. But the closer they got, the tawdrier the town revealed itself to be.

Along the railroad tracks were wagon yards filled with mounds of buffalo hides and great ricks of bleached buffalo bones that had been gathered off the prairies. These would be shipped east and ground into fertilizer for the farmers back there.

There were substantial new buildings fronting the railroad along Front Street, but south of the river was a tent and shanty town, forbidding in its very appearance. A place of bad repute, with gambling, rotgut whiskey and whores.

While Cookie re-provisioned the wagon for the trip south to the Pecos, Elt splurged on a haircut, a bath and a new suit of clothes for his triumphant return home. With spurs ajinglin', he strode the board sidewalks with a newly adopted swagger that he copied from other seasoned cowboys, complete with the gaze and the air of a man sure of himself. He had earned these.

Only a handful of saloons operated north of the tracks and these were tightly marshaled by some of the most feared and respected lawmen of the West. Elt felt little intimidation as he entered the Long Branch Saloon. Just a turn of his head and the look in his eye bid the bartender to pour a drink. This was a far cry from the farm boy on the trail who had watched his fellow drovers carouse in mean bars and cavort with unattractive, even slovenly women.

In this relatively opulent surrounding, he was pleased to be approached by the childlike girl, Meg. This fresh-faced young beauty was certainly out of place in the Long Branch. Her conversation was lively and she found a willing listener in this boy so long on the trail. At a table with this lovely, Elt found himself telling of his adventures with an abandon he had never felt before, and Meg was completely fascinated by him. Although she should have been urging him to buy drinks, she was content just to listen to him.

Her story, of course, fell on believing ears. Coming from the East with a musical troupe, their manager had absconded with all of their money and had abandoned them to their own devices. She had sung in the theatre a time or two, but hadn't earned enough money for the train ticket home to Illinois, her goal in life.

Elt felt good that in surrendering herself to him for a price, he would in fact be helping her flee from this life of sin. He took no note of the ruffian that shadowed them to her room.

Elt had no recollection of from whence the first blow came. But as he awakened next morning in an alley, he knew that ribs were broken, eyes blackened, clothing torn and he didn't even have to feel for his wallet to know that it would be missing.

Meg, with this easy found windfall, had given the slip to her partner and true to her story, was on her way home where she hopefully could leave this sordid life behind. But she would carry the memory of that boy she had robbed for the rest of her life.

It was a chest-fallen Elt who caught up with "Cookie" just as he was preparing to leave Dodge on the trail south to the Pecos. Cookie volunteered to give Elt enough money for a train ticket home. But the remorseful Elt said, "I can't go home now. Not looking like this. Not having anything to show for the months I wasn't there to help them on the farm. Ma would welcome me, but she would know at first glance what my true story was. Ed would be disappointed in me. No. I'll go home after next year's drive".

The ride back across the Cimarron, the Canadian and the Red Rivers, and past Palo Duro and the Staked Plains was an eye opener to Elt, who marveled at the great expanses of grass that would one day be owned by the type of men that he envisioned he would one day become. It was this dream that helped blot out the fiasco at Dodge and the great disappointment that he felt in himself.

When they arrived at the Pecos, there was nothing for Elt to do to earn pay until the roundup for next year's drive that would begin months later. He pledged that he'd be back for the drive and joined several riders headed for Mexico to start collecting a herd.

Elton and Meg at the Long Branch *Illustration by David Cook*

His pay would be his grub and a promise to share in the profits. Brushard, their leader, was quick to supply him with sidearms and a leather jacket and chaps for this rough country of scrub and cacti and thorny brush of all kinds that seemed to reach out for you.

This part of Texas was practically without law, but when they crossed the Rio Grande, they were in a land not known for law or justice, or even civility towards the Yankees. They had been forewarned. The visions of quick profits blinded them.

The four riders Elt had thrown in with were very familiar with this part of Mexico. After crossing the Rio Grande at a well established ford, they left Elt to herd fresh horses for them while they rode on to collect the herd they claimed to have already arranged for.

It was here that Elt was confronted by the local lawman, who called into question the ownership of the horses in his care. Although he had pleaded with him to await the return of the "lawful" owners of the horses, he was unceremoniously thrown into a seedy jail with dirt floors and thick adobe walls in this village with a name not known even a few miles away.

One morning a few days later, a great commotion and lots of gunfire was heard. The jailers simply took off for the brush, leaving the prisoners just that — still prisoners.

From the barred windows of their cells, the prisoners watched as a ragtag mounted troop entered the village plaza and headed straight for the jail. Since the guards had fled in such haste, the cell doors had to be pulled out of their anchorages as the keys to the locks were nowhere to be found.

The prisoners were shouting with joy for their release until they realized they were still prisoners, but now in the sights of riflemen who herded them up against the adobe wall surrounding the jail. The leader of these self-proclaimed "Federalis" rode up on the only saddle horse worthy of the name and with an air of great importance, alighted, straightened out his ill fitting grandly decorated uniform, and advanced toward the cowering prisoners.

"Hombres," he said. "You now have the great privilege of serving in the army of the greatest of all Mexican generals, and fighting for the Revolution! If you will kindly raise your right arm to signify your desire to join this army, you will be enlisted by my sergeant."

By now Elt had learned enough Spanish to catch the drift of what was being offered, and like the other prisoners looking into the barrels of

Elton "Volunteers" for the Mexican Federalis   *Illustration by David Cook*

those rifles and feeling the adobe wall at his back, he wisely decided that enlisting in this ragtag army was his best chance at living one more day.

As a "Gringo", Elt warranted special attention and was always under the watchful eyes of these soldiers---only recently peasants toiling in the fields. But Elt decided his best chance of survival lay with serving his new masters well. When he pointed out the need to trim the hooves of several of the horses, he was put to work in that capacity. He gave special attention to the "General's" fine horse, currying him, rubbing him down, staking him out to graze and leading him to water from time to time.

After a very few days Elt gained the respect of the horsemen. While the other soldiers helped themselves to the goods of the stores and the favors of the locals who had not fled to the hills, he paid attention to details. He even convinced the General that the saddle he was riding needed re-rigging to properly fit such a fine mount.

The other horses were unsaddled and tied to a highline as their riders lounged about in the noonday shade, some in drunken stupor. Elt, swung into the saddle to test the revised rigging and, with a newly acquired knife, cut the highline, thus releasing the haltered horses. He whooped and hollered and drove the frightened horses in front of him and out of the camp.

By now the camp was coming alive with much consternation and swearing and at last, gunfire, as they realized what had happened. Elt realized that it wouldn't be long before some of the scattering horses would drift back into camp, be saddled, and would be in hot pursuit. He rode with great abandon at an all-out gallop toward where he knew the Rio Grande offered him his best hope for escape.

Crossing the river into the United States gave the pursuing Federalis reason to abandon their chase and the brash young man on a very tired saddle horse was given a chance to rest. But not for long.

As he headed north towards the Pecos, he came upon the riders he had crossed into Mexico with. "Frenchy" pulled his gun and threatened Elt for having run off with their horses and when Elt tried to reason with him, Frenchy said, "Shut your damned mouth! I ought to shoot you right here but I'll take you to Brushard and I"ll bet he will find some way to punish you." They were furious with him for not having the fresh horses for them as he had originally been instructed.

Brushard was inclined to believe Elt's story, and after searching him and finding no money that kind of proved Frenchy wrong about Elt having run off with the horses and selling them. The fact that Elt had neither the chaps or the leather jacket, gun or the gloves and hat that he had been outfitted with before going into Mexico reinforced his story. Elt reviewed how the local law recognized one of the horses as having been stolen from him the previous year and it looked as though he might be strung up as a horse thief except that the lawman tended to believe the youngsters story that he was just holding the horses for other riders. Anyway, he was too busy dealing with other matters than to hang the boy right then. There were rumblings that a revolution was underway and his village and the government that he represented might come under attack any day now. Not a pleasant thought for a man unsure of the loyalty or bravery of his underlings.

"I still think you ought to let me shoot the little bastard," taunted Frenchy. "Or at least let me have that saddle horse that he is riding."

"Damn you Frenchy. Just let it drop, and I don't want no more trouble over this, ever!" ordered Brushard.

The herd they were pushing was near exhaustion as were their horses. It was then that Elt noticed the young Mexican boy, tied by the wrists on a pony, who was being brought along as a hostage. He then surmised that this was not a herd of cattle that had been purchased, but that it had been stolen, the owners probably killed, and the boy brought along as a bargaining chip in case they were overtaken.

Chapter 4

Elt immediately felt compassion for this young, terrified Mexican boy. Having witnessed the murder of his parents by this group of ruffians, Jose correctly reasoned that he would meet a similar end when his usefulness as a hostage was over.

Elt convinced Brushard, leader of the ruffians, that the boy would be of little value to them dead. Elt insisted on loosening his bonds and dressing his chafed wrists with bacon grease and wrapping them with soft cotton torn from his shirt tail. He also saw to it that the boy shared his canteen from time to time, helped him mount for the day's ride and helped him dismount and be fed at the end of the day. While he fed the boy, he talked with him using his newly found Spanish words learned in the jail, and with easily understood signing, gained the boy's devotion and loyalty. Elt sought to comfort the child when, at night, bad dreams brought on sobs that he couldn't hide.

They followed a goodly stream into the foothills and finally into a valley in the Santiago Mountains, where the herd could rest and graze for a few days. But always, one of the ruffians was assigned to guard their trail miles behind them in order to give them warning of any pursuit. Well-rested, they began their drive towards the foothills of the Davis Mountains, where they could hold the herd in a broad valley while branding them with a "running brand". In this case, the brand was made with a cinch ring, heated in a hardwood fire and held firmly in the grip of fencing pliers. It would be applied to the left hip of the cattle. The brand was scripted "1T," and papers could be forged to lend legitimacy to the ownership.

The cattle were restrained by one cowboy roping the head and another the hind legs, stretching the animal between the horses and throwing it onto its right side. Two cinch rings were used, one always heating while the other was being applied. Elt convinced Brushard that the boy, Jose, could mind the fire and bring the heated ring to him for the branding. It was evident that the youngster couldn't run off from them, although they did keep his wrists bound when he was not at work under their supervision.

Jose, the Hostage   *Illustration by David Cook*

After four days of intensive "cowboyin'" the herd was branded and moved into a canyon with steep ridges on each side to hide for a few weeks. It was important to let the brands age before heading on to the Pecos and the spring trail drive.

By now, they were nearly out of food and Brushard decided that Elt was the logical one to send to the nearest settlement that they had studiously avoided. This was partly because he would not be as likely to be recognized as the others, who were not unknown in these parts. Frenchy asked for that job, but Brushard rightly reasoned, "They probably have your picture in the post office and anyways, you'd just get drunk and ferget what the hell you was supposed to be doin'".

Elt was dispatched on this errand with instructions as to how much beans, flour, bacon and canned fruits to buy, and hopefully, there would be money enough left for a bottle or two of whiskey. The saloonkeepers wouldn't question the age of this boy, or where his money had come from.

Here was the opportunity for Elt to escape from these ruffians. But the escape plan took on a devious twist when Elt reasoned that he might not only escape, but that he might acquire the herd as his own!

Instead of buying all of the groceries he had been sent for, Elt bought only a small supply. With the remainder of the money, he purchased four cheap six-shooters and lots of ammunition. As he crested the ridge overlooking the campsite, Elt could make out that every one of the ruffians was near the campfire. He dismounted and tied his horse a safe distance away and then laid out all four of the loaded pistols on a downed log. Elt took a deep breath and then proceeded to fire the pistols as fast as he could into the trees above the campsite. He watched with a knowing smile as the ruffians jumped to their feet, found their horses and headed out through the timber at breakneck speed to escape the imagined "posse" that surely was hot on their trail. They had left Jose bound and tied to a tree.

Brushard had been taking a "sponge bath" and was stripped to the waist when the fusillade erupted. He was not interested in retrieving his brocade-front vest with its gold watch and watch chain and inner money pocket that could only be accessed by unbuttoning the vest. The vest, watch and chain had most certainly been taken from one of his victims. Brushard led the retreat bare chested into the night.

Satisfied that the rustlers had been driven off and would not soon rein-in in their flight, Elt rode into camp and took the bindings from a grateful Jose. At age seventeen, Elt now had his own herd and a trustworthy new compadre. He appropriated the vest, gold watch and chain as his own. At sunrise, well fed, they drove the herd out of the canyon and headed north through the foothills. They knew that within days they would surely reach the river above Pecos, and when the time was right, they would join the trail herd being assembled by Colonel Rice.

Then one day, leaving the herd under the care of Jose, Elt rode into Pecos and enlisted the aid of "Dusty" Rhodes, a competent drover from last year's trail drive. With Elt and Dusty doing the roping, it was an easy task for Jose to cross the "1" of the "1T" brand and turn it into a "TT" brand. It would be an easy matter to obtain ownership papers for the "TT" herd.

When Elt brought his herd onto the plain north of Pecos to join the trail herd, he made no effort to hide the identity of the "TT" brand from Colonel Rice, and told him all of the details of his adventures since last seeing him in Miles City. The Colonel was astounded, and more than a little disappointed, in hearing of the Dodge City fiasco. But he was also understanding and perfectly willing to have this valued drover with him for the coming drive.

Elt sold the yearling steers and heifers to the Colonel. This money would be his "grub stake". He agreed to join the drive at no pay in return for including his bulls, cows and calves in the drive until he would choose to leave the drive with his small herd in the Powder River country of Wyoming Territory. There he hoped to establish his own ranch.

Jose became like a shadow to Elt. Eager to learn all that he could from this young accomplished horseman, he assumed more and more responsibility in the care and feeding of the saddle horses. He was most anxious to please Elt, and a smile or nod of appreciation was the only reward he needed.

The combination of Elt and Jose became a great asset to Colonel Rice as they could converse and interpret in bargaining with the several Mexican ranchers in the area who had stock to sell. The square dealings that resulted from these understandings put the colonel in an advantageous position in dealing with other stock owners as word of his good reputation spread.

Jose would continue with the drive until it reached its destination. Then his half-pay would be entrusted to Cookie, who would bring Jose back to Pecos and maybe on to his home in Mexico.

Chapter 5

The trail herd was assembled over a period of a month as cattle were drifted in from almost every direction. It required slowly moving the assemblage a mile at a time to fresh grasses on the wide Pecos plains. Bullers and other problem cattle had to be sorted off and reintroduced into the herd days later. The entire growing herd had to be continuously circled and formed into a cohesive unit before starting out on the long drive north.

Cookie had arrived with the newly repaired and outfitted chuck and bed wagon. Jose would come along at only a one-half pay, but he was glad to be with Elt and to learn the lessons as a helper to the "horse jingler", Tommy Aikens.

Easy ten-mile days were the rule at the outset, until fatigue began to set in and the natural born leaders took up their place at the head of the drive — a spot they would not willingly give up for the remainder of the journey. As the days wore on, it was evident that the natural leader was a four-year-old Longhorn/Hereford cross steer, with horns over four feet from tip to tip. Of gentle behavior, he had a quieting effect on the younger, spooky cattle. First to bed down at the end of the day and the last to rise in the morning, he given the name "Champ." From the very start, he would not give up his role as leader until the herd was dispersed to the Indian agencies.

Elt and Dusty took turns at point and alternated scouting ahead for the night's bed-ground and water sources as a reward for being exceptionally savvy drovers, already proven on the previous year's drive. Colonel Rice was comfortable with turning over more and more responsibility to these exceptional drovers.

The trail herd consisted of nearly three thousand, three- and four-year-old steers, plus the eighty head of cows, calves, and bulls belonging to Elt. The steers were destined to be distributed to Indian tribes in Montana and the North and South Dakota territories as part of the government contracts.

Early on the during the drive around the evening's campfires, Elt convinced the colonel that Jose should return with "Cookie" after the drive was over and that his pay should be entrusted to Cookie until they were back at Pecos. Then, every effort would be made to help Jose return to his home in Mexico. That met with only partial agreement from Jose who couldn't imagine life without the companionship and direction of Elt.

The route of the drive would be far west of the previous year's drive as homesteaders had pushed further and ever further west. In central Wyoming, it became each drover's duty to haze Elt's cattle to the rear of the herd and when, at last, it was time for Elt to quit the drive, his cattle were already bonding and comfortable going off on a separate route. That would be toward the foothills of the Little Bighorns, where great expanses of grasses were not, as yet, being reclaimed after the blizzard of '86 that had decimated the herds. Only a few of the ranches settled before "The Big Dieup" were still in existence. Many homesteaders were wiped out and abandoned their homesteads and headed for more hospitable country.

Leaving the drive was much more difficult than Elt had imagined. Cookie and Dusty, but most of all the Colonel and Jose made saying goodbye an emotional thing that Elt had not counted on. The tearful Jose wanted to leave with Elt, but Elt persuaded him to stay with the drive.

Colonel Rice rode with Elt for a couple of hours before he could at last say goodbye.

"Elt, I think that the days of the great cattle drives are coming to an end and I will probably return to what remains of my plantation and I'll try to rebuild it," Said Colonel Rice. "There is reason to believe that we will probably never see one another again. I wish that I had had more men like you under my command during the war."

Both men teared up as the Colonel turned his horse, Pride, to rejoin the drive. Elt suddenly felt terribly alone and questioned his own decisions before pressing on to the west.

Elt was riding his favorite mount, "Blaze," the blazed-faced, four-year-old sorrel gelding that he had appropriated from the ragtag Mexican General. Formerly named "El Capitan," Elt had renamed the horse "Blaze" shortly after coming back across the Rio Grande. He also took another horse, "Heesa", from the remuda and tied panniers to his saddle to carry the staples he would be needing in the coming months while he was setting up his ranch. "Cookie" could spare only a little of those staples from the drive's supply. Elt was on his own, as never before in his life.

CHAPTER 6

The peaks of the Little Big Horns were just barely discernable on the western horizon when Elt started his small herd towards their new home. The grasses on the prairie at the foothills of the mountain were practically ungrazed since the great herds of cattle were decimated in the recent "Big Die-Up," the unprecedented blizzard that had paralyzed the high plains from Texas to the British (Canada). Elt made careful note of several abandoned homesteads that he might take for the headquarters of the ranch he had dreamed of, and was well on his way to realizing.

One abandoned homestead not many miles from the KC Ranch and the Bozeman Trail really caught his eye. It was in the shelter of a sharp hill with several mature trees and a lively stream running past the corral. It would not take a lot of work to repair the corral fence and make it usable again. Elt would check this out again when he came down off the mountain later in the summer.

Heesa and Blaze had buddied up to the point that Elt no longer needed the lead rope on Heesa's halter and he realized that, not content to just tag along, Heesa was beginning to help work the drag and keep the laggards pushed up and moving — an inherent instinctive thing that couldn't have been taught. It is known as "horse sense".

Working upstream on what proved to be the Powder River, the herd kept doggedly pushing to the west and ignored the several tributaries. They crossed the Bozeman Trail and on past the KC ranch, one of only a few still in existence. Elt encountered few riders and there was no opportunity to re-supply his meager cache of foodstuffs. These, he would have to use sparingly. He would have to be a hunter and a gatherer to survive.

Once through the gap in the Red Wall that stretches nearly seventy miles north and south in central Wyoming territory, the drive became just a controlled grazing operation as they drifted higher, ever higher, up the mountainside to the broad high meadows. Here, life would be easier. Although the herd must be kept gathered up, there was no reason for the cattle to stray off. It was a simple time of grazing, drinking from the numerous streams and lying down in the warm, late summer sun. Prairie fowl and antelope were plentiful and there was no reason to take a "maybe" shot, as Elt carefully rationed his ammunition and could afford to wait for the "sure" shot.

He had observed the Indians hanging thin strips of meat on tree limbs to dry and this talent he carefully developed, knowing that it would be invaluable later on. Elt built a bow of willow using a tendon string to operate as a twirling firemaking instrument that he would need, keeping it secure in his saddle bag. The instrument took Elt hours to develop, but since there was so little demand on his time, he painstakingly crafted it as a trustworthy, precision instrument, a replacement for matches or steel-striking flint.

As the chokecherry "fire stick" was twirled against a piece of dead cottonwood, enough heat would be generated to fire dry grasses. Elt realized that he was constantly gathering "fire sticks" and hoarding them in his saddlebag; more than he could possibly have a use for. He became aware of other traits. He had always talked a lot to his horses, but now he realized that he often stopped as though awaiting a reply of some sort. Elt also realized that he was talking out loud to himself more and more.

"I must stop this," He thought. "I may be going crazy. I need to see some other human beings."

One feature of the grazing area was the presence of hundreds of "Tipi Rings." They were circles of rock that at one time had held down the edges of a tipi and were left in place when the tipi was moved. These always seemed to be on high broad plateaus where the tipis could have been seen for miles away. The Indians that had lived here evidently had felt no need to hide their presence.

Another puzzling aspect of the location of the tipi rings was their distance from water. In some cases water for drinking or cooking would have to have been carried nearly a mile. But as those sorts of chores fell to the womenfolk it evidently wasn't much of a deal! In the firepits near where the tipis had been, Elt found small smooth but porous stones. These evidently were easily heated and gave up their heat readily when dropped into a pot of a liquid based food to heat it. He soon learned to utilize them that way also.

The long warm summer afternoons gave Elt lots of time to think about the value of things. His gold watch, that he had prized, had little value out here. It just wasn't important to know what time it was. It just didn't matter. He thought of the stick pin that the banker back home wore. It was said to be a diamond. Out here, who the hell would be impressed with a diamond? And that was what it was all about, to impress.

The things of real value to him were his hatchet and his skinning knife.

Elt knew full well the absolute need to get down off the mountain before the first snow. But the early fall was so mild, and things were going so well with the herd, that he hesitated to break the spell. He had built a small brush-covered ramada that he further covered with a wagon sheet to protect himself from the showers that seemed to develop so regularly these autumn afternoons.

The first inkling he had of the great tragedy that was about to befall him was when he was awakened from a deep sleep by the sound of a splintering tree branch breaking under the weight of a heavy snowfall that he hadn't been aware of. The previous evening had just a hint of fall cool in the air, but under a full moon and a cloudless sky, he had fallen asleep contentedly. In the dark of night, and with the snow still falling, there was little he could do until daylight came and the snowfall abated. He then realized that it was a matter of life or death to get down off of the mountain as fast as possible, and he gathered all his gear together in the saddle panniers that Heesa would carry.

It was a wet snow that already reached nearly a foot deep when just before daylight the wind came up with a sudden roar like that of a freight train rumbling by, and in the blowing snow there was nothing to be done until the wind died down and it became light.

That would not happen for another twenty-four hours. As the temperature plummeted, Elt tore down part of the brush ramada and fired it to keep from freezing to death. He paid attention to the adage his Pa had often quoted, "White man build big fire and sit way back, but Indian builds little fire and sits up close"! From the canvas wagon sheet that had covered the ramada, Elt cut a strip to serve as a scarf that he tied over his hat and ears and tied under his chin. He then double-folded the rest of the canvas sheet and cut a hole in the center thus fashioning a poncho that he so desperately needed. He was beginning to think that this is how it might all end — that he would die here within days of the time when he thought he was about to realize his life's dream of owning his own spread.

At last the wind died down, the black clouds scurried off and the brightest sunshine he had ever witnessed took over. It was difficult to see. The

Elt and Blaze Breach a Snowdrift   Illustration by David Cook

surface of the white snow from horizon to horizon was melting on its surface and then freezing. It turned the whole landscape into one limitless mirror. A wide-brimmed hat might protect your eyes from the sun overhead, but nothing could protect them from the glare being reflected off the surface of the snow. Not even squinting could totally keep the eyes from searing, and Elt realized he was becoming painfully sunburned about his face, the only part of his body not protected. He drew a bandana over his ears and cheeks, leaving the barest slit to look out from.

His horses were still tied close at hand, and a surprising number of cattle were still huddled in the small patch of pinion-pine where they had bedded down before the storm.

The snow had been swept from stretches of ground maybe one hundred yards long and then deposited in waist-high drifts. The drifts ranged from one side of a deep canyon on the north, maybe two hundred yards, to an equally steep canyon to the south. A person or a cow brute or a horse would break though the frozen crust of ice with each step. And even Blaze could not lunge through the wide windrow of a drift before he would flounder and almost give up. Elt found that he could clamber on foot through the drift and slog back though his trail to the other side to lead Blaze back and forth through the track until it was packed enough to drive his remaining cattle through single-file. There was thought of trying to round up the missing cattle, but that thought quickly evaporated when he realized how perilous his situation had become. Once through that first drift, Elt could see that there was a series of drifts about one hundred yards apart all of the way down the mountainside between these two sharp canyons, not unlike the steps of a ladder lying down. At the end of the first day, they had only traversed three drifts and he was totally exhausted. But there was still only one hope of survival---that was to keep breaching these snowdrifts and get off of the mountain.

On the second day Elt took time to make a small fire, cook a small meal and melt snow to drink. Horses can eat snow to take care of their needs but cattle have never developed that capability. When the last windrow of snow was breeched, it led them into a grove where a small stream was still flowing. The cattle piled over one another in their mad dash to quench their thirst, and several were injured to the extent that they could no longer keep up.

On the morning of the fourth day, Elt awakened with excruciating pain in his eyes. He could not distinguish a cow critter from a small bush, and he could not locate Heesa with the only food supply. Elt had been snow-blinded and he was far from being saved, even after all they had gone through. On Blaze, once more, he tried to push what cattle he could find to follow that little stream out onto the plains, maybe cross the Bozeman Trail and find help.

When help did arrive, it was not what he had hoped for. The three "Good Samaritans" who discovered him told Elt that Chuck Cable would lead him to Fort Casper to see the post doctor, and that Adam Slaughter and John Baker would hold his herd for him just south of Buffalo where there was still grass not snow covered. He could recover the herd whenever he was again capable of tending them.

Actually, they had decided to take his small herd as their own and Chuck was instructed to take Elt off to the side, kill him and take his gun and his horse.

Chuck Cable was not capable of such a dastardly murder. He struck Elt over the head with his own gun and left him to die on the prairie. He then took Elt's gun and Blaze. But he told Slaughter and Baker that he had carried out the deed. He had even fired Elt's pistol twice into the air so that his cohorts might hear, and assume that Elt had been killed. He hadn't bothered to search Elt for valuables such as his gold watch. He was too sick realizing that he had been a party to such an offense.

Chapter 7

"God damned dog," grumbled Joe Spivak as he reigned his teams to a halt. Joe was freighting goods from Fort Laramie to the suttlers store in Fort Kearney. His rig was two freight wagons, tied together and pulled by eight draft horses in ranges of twos. Melting of the early fall snow had turned the road into a nearly impossible mud quagmire. He was already two days behind his usual schedule and he contemplated stopping at KC ranch to see if he could buy grain for his teams; his supply was nearly used up already. He had debated dropping off the tag wagon and going on. But with no way to protect it from thieves he decided just to slug on.

"Sport," the young dog of questionable ancestry, often ranged far off of the trail in search of a good chase or even adventure. Today he ignored Joe's whistle and continued to run in circles, barking and trying to summon him. Joe climbed down from the lead freight wagon after setting the brake — hardly needed, but done out of habit. He carried his shotgun and muttered, "If you've run another skunk to ground, I may just shoot you, Sport."

But what Joe discovered was a mud-covered young man with blood-matted hair, barely conscious. It was soon evident to Joe that the watery bloodshot eyes belonged to a man who was snow-blinded and hallucinatory. He was asking about his cattle and his horse. After dragging the nearly dead young man over to his wagon, and with great effort was able to lift him over the tailgate of the lead wagon. He returned for his shotgun and looked around for any clue to the circumstances leading up to this man's condition. There were tracks of two horses leading to and from the spot where he was found.

Joe stopped by the KC ranch where they bathed the young man, bandaged his wound, dried his clothing, fed him and questioned him about the incident. One of the KC cowboys identified Elt as the man who had drifted about eighty head of cattle past the ranch maybe ninety days before. "He was riding a magnificent saddle horse," the cowboy remembered.

Next stop for Joe was past the store and bar at Big Horn, where he left Elt in their care until his return trip. He deemed Elt too weak to continue on.

Joe carefully opened and removed just a few pounds of dry beans, or flour, or coffee beans from each of the many one hundred pound sacks he was to deliver to Ft. Kearney. These he gave to the saloonkeeper and carefully retied the pilfered sacks. Joe hoped that the men that the storekeeper would hire to unload his wagon would not notice the shrinkage. Maybe he could keep them entertained with ribald jokes he had heard at Ft. Casper and thus divert their attention.

Harry Stein, the owner, bartender and cook, found that Elt could wash dishes and earn his keep as his strength slowly returned. After a couple of months of this, Harry gave Elt a pistol and gun belt and holster that Elt had showed much interest in. Harry didn't comprehend how Elt could use a pistol when he could hardly see. He didn't recognize the sharpening sense of sound and direction that Elt was developing.

Jose, after a long search for his friend and mentor, learned of Elt's whereabouts from the cowboys at KC ranch. He followed the trail first to Ft. Kearney and then back to Big Horn, where he took over the care of his friend.

Harry was glad to enlist the services of Jose to help cook for the occasional travelers who stopped in.

Jose quickly endeared himself to Harry and to the regulars that he would call by name the second time they met. The regulars were flattered by the recognition and took delight at the speech inflections of this young Mexican boy. Harry was addressed as "Mister Hair-ree" and Dick was called "Mister Deek". Soon the regulars were laughing and calling each other by their new names.

Jose had convinced Cookie that he should have his pay from the drive so that he could find Elt and join him in the ranching plans. After all, he had no family to return to in Mexico and the thought of returning to the farm where he had witnessed the killing of his parents was not one that he wanted to experience.

He bought satisfactory clothing for Elt, and was encouraging him to eat more and concentrate on getting stronger. The bar was the warmest place around and they spread their suggans on the floor at the end of each evening's business.

Late one evening three men stomped in demanding drink and food in loud overbearing shouts. Harry set a bottle and three glasses on the crude bar in front of them and went back to the kitchen to prepare some food.

Elt was seated at a table in the far corner of the room, and as the cobwebs cleared from his brain, he recognized the three by their voices as the men who had stolen his herd and horse and gun and left him for dead out on the prairie.

As their eyes became adjusted to the dim light of the single lantern, Adam, who was standing at the end of the bar, looked in disbelief at the man sitting in the far corner. "God almighty, Chuck! There is the feller you claimed you had killed, so you better do the job right now."

Jose had just come in from the kitchen as both Adam and Chuck were drawing their guns.

"Kill the lantern!" Elt shouted to Jose in Spanish, and the room was plunged into absolute darkness.

Shots rang out from the men at the bar and the man in the corner. Elt had overturned his table and was using it as a shield. "Oh, God! I've been hit!" screamed Chuck, as more shots were fired.

"Shut up you damned fool! He's shooting at the sound of your voice!"

At least that's what Adam was trying to warn when he stopped in mid-sentence and was not heard from again as his life's blood spread on the wooden floor.

John Baker made a mad dash out the door and stopped to unload his pistol back into the room before taking off. Chuck had taken a second slug and was never to complain again. After the shooting died down, Harry came into the bar carrying a lantern and trying to discern what had gone on. Through the haze of gunsmoke, the dim light revealed Adam splayed out at the end of the bar and Chuck draped over a crude chair. Both were dead. Gradually, he could make out Elt crouched behind the overturned table where he had been sitting. He was unscratched.

"Jose, Jose, are you alright?" Elt frantically called out.

There was no reply.

Harry discovered Jose behind the bar, a victim of the wild shots that Baker had unleashed as he rushed out of the door.

As the shock of Jose having been killed wore off, Harry turned Adam over and took a closer look at him.

"God almighty, Elt! You've killed the sheriff's son, Adam! He has always been a no good son of a bitch, but he was the apple of his father's eye."

"You've got to get the hell out of here as fast and as far as you can. It don't matter that Adam deserved to die. The sheriff will try to follow you to the ends of the earth to get revenge."

Harry had to shake Elt to get his attention and to convince him of the gravity of his situation and he nearly had to physically shove him out of the tavern to get him on his way.

"We'll give Jose a proper burial," Harry pledged to the grieving Elt. But you have to get the hell out of here as fast as you can and as far as you can."

Outside the tavern, Harry and Elt checked out the three horses still tied at the rail.

More by instinct than feel, Elt realized that one of the horses was his beloved Blaze, and he chose him to make good his escape.

"I can't help you much Elt. But maybe you can follow the creek out onto the plains. I won't report these killings to the sheriff 'til I have to, but I'll bet Baker is going to." Baker had left in such a panic that he didn't even take his horse; he just wanted to disappear into the night.

"You will be wanted for murder and for horse stealing," warned Harry.

Once more on his trusty Blaze, Elt was following a stream only by its sound out onto the prairie with a single canteen of water and a bundle of food hastily put together by Harry before Elt left Big Horn in the middle of the night. Once again he was riding for his life.

The light snow that had begun to fall was, in reality, a godsend as after only a few hours it would make tracking him impossible.

Chapter 8

Having spent the last two months in the relative warmth of the Big Horn Saloon, Elt was in no condition to be riding in the bitter cold of the Wyoming winter. Blaze soon learned the escape plan, and would follow near the banks of Piney Creek out onto the plains with little guidance. From time to time Elt had to alight and walk until his feet would be warm enough to re-mount

All of the time he was grieving for his Mexican friend, Jose, who had worshipped him and depended upon him and wanted nothing more from life than to please him and to be with him.

When daylight came, Elt felt compelled to put as many miles behind him as possible and rode on knowing well that he might be spotted and reported. He had wrapped a bandana around his neck and over his eyes to protect them from the bright sunlight, only peeking out occasionally to assure himself that Blaze was taking him farther and farther away from Big Horn. Elt knew the reputation of Sheriff Slaughter as a bully, given easily to uncontrollable rages and to pistol-whipping helpless men. The loss of his son would surely bring out the worst in the man.

Blaze forded the occasional tributaries that flowed into Piney Creek and stayed with the larger flow until it joined the Powder. Just at nightfall of that first day, they came to a clearing where the winds had swept the snow from the tall dry grass. Even that dry grass was welcomed by the near worn out Blaze. But Elt dare not start a fire to warm himself, and he walked in circles stamping his feet and flailing his arms in an effort to warm himself.

Long before daylight Elt felt that Blaze might be rested enough to continue the flight. It was essential that they travel slowly enough that Blaze not break into a sweat in this frigid weather.

At the end of the second day, they arrived at a small stand of timber and Elt knew he had to build a fire to warm himself to survive, in spite of the possibility of giving away his location. Water had not been a problem, as both he and Blaze could drink from the river. But Elt had to be extra cautious not to fall in or to even step into the water, as hypothermia would surely doom him.

Next morning there was bright sunshine and a welcome and relatively warm breeze came up from out of the south. Elt realized that he was getting weaker and he had begun to cough a cough that shook his entire frame. At one point, he dismounted and was sitting down, bent over from a coughing seizure, when fate once more intervened.

Little Thunder and Smiling Boy from the band once ruled by Old Running Horse were out on their ponies exploring on this first warm day of the season, and they cautiously rode up closer to the sick man sitting on the ground. He was a pitiful sight, but even the fatigued Blaze was one of the most magnificent horses they had ever seen. They considered just waiting the dying man out and then taking his horse.

Elt judged from the rapt attention that Blaze was displaying, and more by instinct than by sound or by sight, he was aware of the boys' presence. Then hearing just a bit of their conversation and recognizing the language, he struggled to his feet, raised an arm in salute and in a harsh voice said, "I am WhiteElk, a friend of Old Running Horse!"

The boys were so taken aback at being addressed in their own language and they looked to one another for some sort of direction. Their first thoughts were to race back to camp and tell of their discovery. They then decided that it was more important to take the man back to camp with them. After introducing themselves to Elt, they helped the near helpless man into his saddle and rode on each side of Blaze, actually rubbing against him as they needed to keep Elt from falling out of the saddle.

There was much confusion in the camp as they rode in with this white man in their keep. They were greeted just outside of his tipi by Young Running Horse, who had taken over as leader of this band since the death of Old Running Horse, his father, just this past summer.

Elt was so weak he was nearly incoherent, but he was able to blurt out, "I am WhiteElk, friend of Old Running Horse!" What followed was almost like a dream.

He was aware that he had been taken into a tipi. He was aware that his right sleeves had been drawn back to expose the long white scar. He was dimly aware of hearing the exclamation, "This truly is WhiteElk, the savior of my father, who fed the tribe at the Platte!" Elt passed out for a long time.

When consiousness finally did return, he realized that for the first time in a long time he was truly warm, wrapped up in a buffalo robe, and that someone was trying to get him to swallow a warm broth. He could sense the presence of many people in the tipi from the murmurs when he at last opened his eyes. And the gasps as they realized that this young man was snowblind.

In the days that followed and as sensibility slowly returned, Elt realized that the warm broth was gradually being replaced by a meaty stew that was being hand-fed to him. Passing in and out of consciousness, he was only able to smile and mumble a thank you in appreciation for this care.

Whenever Elt would ask for water, he was given a warm brew of herbs by an old woman whom he came to know as a healer. As a woman, she could not be considered a medicine man, but she was very learned in the art of natural cures. He became aware that moist patches were periodically being placed over his closed eyelids. In the light of day, Elt was able to discern that the patches were being gummed and replaced from time to time by what he perceived to be the most beautiful young woman he had ever seen. He judged that the soft leather patches were releasing their tannin by action of the saliva. The patches were discarded after three applications, and new ones applied in their place.

As Elt regained strength and was beginning to become more alert, Young Running Horse led him to know that the young girl was the widow of Grey Horse, his son. At the proper time, Grey Horse would have assumed his place as head of the band and would have received the new name, "Young Running Horse" while Young Running Horse would have become "Old Running Horse." But Grey Horse, a fearless rider, was killed during a buffalo hunt.

Young Running Horse had placed the beautiful widow, Red Sky Woman, in charge of Elt's recovery. She was the woman that Young Running Horse had hoped would be the mother of his grandson, a future leader. But Red Sky Woman had not conceived a child.

The gentle manner and gracious appreciation for every courtesy by this young white man soon won the undying allegiance of Red Sky Woman, and she tried ever harder to please him and to help speed his recovery.

When Elt was strong enough to stand and walk, he and Red Sky Woman left the shelter of the tipi in the darkening of evening. Elt asked about the whereabouts of his saddle horse, Blaze. Red Sky Woman called for Young Running Horse to tell him.

Red Sky Woman Ministers to the Snowblind Elt   *Illustration by David Cook*

It seems that lawmen had visited the camp asking if anyone knew of the near blind man who was wanted for murder. Of course, no one admitted to having seen anyone of that description. Discovery of their deception would have led to disastrous retribution upon the entire tribe.

Knowing that the sighting of such a magnificent horse as Blaze would arouse suspicions and bring questions, Young Running Horse had had him slaughtered and his hide burned along with the saddle, the saddle blanket, and the headstall, and the bit was deep buried. The initial shock of this revelation nearly brought out a rage in Elt. Then he pondered the reasoning of the act and in as much nothing could now be done about it, Elt cooled down. Then the thought that some of the warm meaty stew he had been fed might have come from Blaze almost made him gag.

Whenever a stranger would approach the camp, Elt would be led back into the tipi. There were frequent visitors to the tipi. Primarily it was the young women who wanted to hear the ticking of his time machine and to watch the progress of the hands. Older women gossiped that the young white man might in fact be a "spirit man." That did not escape the attention of Young Running Horse who also resented the hours that Little Thunder and Smiling Boy spent trying to learn more about the white mans' life from Elt. But his obligation to this young white man kept Young Running Horse from putting a stop to these visits.

As the weeks went by and the early spring nights were still cold, Red Sky Woman shared Elts' bed. She would become the only woman that he ever loved.

Red Sky Woman lovingly called Elt "Elk," and in return he affectionately called her simply "Woman."

In the warm spring afternoons, Elt began to think about returning to the white man's world, and not imposing himself any longer upon his red hosts. He sensed that he was wearing out his welcome with Young Running Horse. He could now see pretty well, but his eyes would be bloodshot and watery all of the remaining days of his life.

When he shared the possibility of leaving the tribe, Red Sky Woman told him that she was getting heavy with his child.

Elt quickly changed his mind and volunteered that he would stay with the tribe and live as a red man. Red Sky Woman appreciated the offer, but she had listened to the aspirations of this young white man and knew that in time he would weary of the red man's life and might be resentful. She asked that Elt take her with him.

Elt knew of the stigma that would follow him as a Squawman. It would make employment very difficult in the white man's world. Yet he was so thrilled at the prospect of being a father that he could not think of leaving Red Sky Woman behind.

Young Running Horse was at first aghast at the thought of Red Sky Woman leaving the tribe. As a final gesture of thankfulness to this young man who had saved his father, Old Running Horse, he outfitted them with two saddle horses and supplies to last several days. He did not give them his blessing.

As they rode off towards the south on an early morning, the whole camp, less Young Running Horse, came out to wave and cheer Whitelk and Red Sky Woman as these two had become their favorites. Little Thunder and Smiling Boy rode with them for most of that first day before bidding them "fare thee well" and turning back towards their camp. Red Sky Woman could not hold back her tears as she wondered if she would ever see her family again. Life as a squawman had begun for Elt.

Chapter 9

The first day's ride was a quiet one, as each mile took Red Sky Woman farther and farther away from her family and her tribe. Elt understood her concerns and he did not press her for conversation or inquire of her thoughts. He was letting her sort out her feelings as only she was capable of doing. The first night they camped in a grove alongside a small watercourse. They cooked their evening meal over a small flickering fire and then went to bed. The ponies were tied to a lariat highline between two trees, with enough lead rope that they could graze a swath about ten feet wide with no chance of becoming entangled in the rope.

That night, under a starlit sky, Red Sky Woman came to grips with her situation, and in a moment of illumination, she heaved a sigh of relief and snuggled more closely to Elt, resolving not to cry any more. She spoke softly of her love for him and how excited she was to be starting her new life with such a considerate man. It was a night of great joy, and Elt began to look forward to his life with this beautiful young girl, and smiling at the thought of being a father.

They talked at length about what they might name their child. Inasmuch as they would be living in a white man's world, they agreed that they should give their child a white man's name. Since there might be wanted posters out for Elt's arrest, they decided that henceforth he would go under the name of Bill Williams. If the child were a boy, Bill wanted to name him "Ed," after his beloved brother, and Red Sky Woman was perfectly agreeable to his wishes. They also agreed to the name of "Elizabeth" if the child were a girl. Bill rolled the name over and over on his tongue; Elizabeth Williams! Elizabeth Williams! Elizabeth Williams! They were ecstatic about the idea, and as much in love as two young people could possibly be.

The stark reality of their situation was soon evident. They had provisions for only a few days and it was essential that Bill find work. After three days ride, they came to an area of the plains of the Powder recently homesteaded. Out here, the river was always referred to as just the Powder, never the Powder River.

At the first few homesteads they stopped to apply for work, there wasn't enough work for a hired man; and if there was, there wasn't a place for a squawman. They were treated with disdain. Bill deeply resented this, but he was in no position to show the offense that it gave him.

Finally they came to the homestead of George and Helen Thompson up on Nine-Mile Wash. George had suffered a broken leg when he had a runaway with the team he was driving and the wagon had overturned. The few acres of cultivated farmland were in need of plowing in preparation for spring planting and he needed help, even if the help was from a squawman. George had bought up several of the other homesteads that were offered him at very reasonable prices after they had been "proved up" and the homesteaders wanted to return to the East or to just move on. The shanty on one of these homesteads was just a mile and a half away from the Thompsons, and it would serve as home for Bill and Red Sky Woman.

The only child of George and Helen was an eight-year-old boy called "Tommy". Tommy was more fascinated with, than afraid of, this hardworking young man and his squaw, the most beautiful girl he had ever seen. Helen was a devout Christian and made every effort to help Bill and this girl, whom she did not consider to be a heathen, make a home for themselves — especially after a couple of months when it became evident that Red Sky Woman was with child.

The shanty was fundamentally a sound board and batten house measuring eight feet by sixteen feet, with no interior walls or plaster. The roof did not leak, and there was a functional heating and cooking stove. The only broken window pane was easily boarded over. Although there was no bed, Red Sky Woman and Bill preferred sleeping under the stars on these warm summer nights.

Bill was astonished each evening when he would ride back to their home at the improvements Red Sky Woman had made. First, the entire house had been washed down and washed out, and then kept dust-free with the aid of a broom she had crafted from slough grasses. Then there were the backrests made from willow branches, laced together with leather whang. There were plentious antelope for meat and the hides were cured and then tanned by some process that Red Sky Woman knew.

There were some perennial vegetables from a previous garden that she discovered and cultivated, along with vegetables they shared from the garden of the Thompsons. Life was good.

Bill had an aversion to going into the nearest town. He would harness the team to the spring wagon for George and Helen to take shopping and they would buy what clothing and dry goods and anything else the hired couple might be needing. They would pay for these items with money from Bill's wages that he never asked for. Life was good.

In the months that followed, the acre of potatoes was harvested and stored in the root cellar. The five acres of corn provided enough hominy to last the coming year, and the fodder helped winter the cows. The cows produced way too much milk for the two families' consumption, so the excess was churned into butter and the skimmed milk was used to slop the pigs. The pigs provided bacon and hams, and the intestines were cleaned to form casings for the sausages. The five acres of wheat provided enough grain to grind into flour to last the next year. Life was good.

As George's broken leg healed, he could spend more and more time helping with the gardening and the milking of the cows. At one point, George felt strong enough to take a team and wagon to a coal mine near Sheridan and buy a winter's supply of coal for heating and cooking. There was a near absence of any timber in the area to heat with. George was puzzled by Bill's reluctance to leave the farm, but accepted it without undue questioning.

The daily routine was something like this: In the early morning, Bill and Red Sky Woman would breakfast together and then Bill would catch up his horse and ride over to the Thompson's headquarters. There, he would milk the three or four cows and turn them out to graze. He would then plow, plant, cultivate and care for whatever crops needed his attention. He took his noon meal with the Thompsons, and unlike their former hired hands, he would always take his dishes and silverware from the table and help Helen with the dishes. He was always sure that there was coal in the scuttle to make her chores a little easier.

An hour before sundown, Bill would saddle up and bring in the cows for the night. After milking, Bill would take only enough milk to provide for the following day and ride back to his home at sunset. He never ceased to wonder at the great thrill he experienced when Red Sky Woman would greet him as he rode in. After he had unsaddled and turned his horse out to graze in a small pasture trap, a warm meal would be awaiting him. The night would be spent entwined in one another's arms, as they spoke of their dreams of the future before drifting off to sleep. Life was good.

In the late fall, as the leaves were falling from the few trees to announce the coming of winter, Bill rode in at nightfall one evening but wasn't met by Red Sky Woman. He was puzzled at this turn of events as he unsaddled his horse and turned him loose into the pasture trap. There was no light from the lantern, and when Bill tried to open the door there was pressure against it. In desperation, he broke out a window to gain entrance to his home. He called out to Red Sky Woman and heard only moans in response. He lit a lantern and found Red Sky Woman lying in front of the door, nearly unconscious and bleeding profusely. She was well into childbirth, well ahead of the anticipated time.

Bill tried to comfort Red Sky Woman, but he realized that he was ill prepared to assist. He caught up his horse and in a wild ride in the gathering darkness he rode to the Thompson's for help. His horse stepped into a hole, fell and rolled over him, breaking his right leg and several ribs. The horse was uninjured, and took off leaving Bill near unconscious with a broken leg, a mile from help.

An hour before sunrise, George and Helen were awakened by the insistant barking of their dog. Lighting a lantern, George went out into the yard to see what the commotion was all about. There he found Bill, dragging himself towards the house and pleading for help for Red Sky Woman. George and Helen left Bill in the care of Tommy, while George harnessed the team to the spring wagon and he and Helen raced to the cabin of Bill and Red Sky Woman.

They were too late. There was nothing they could do. Both Red Sky Woman and the child who was to have been named Elizabeth were dead.

George enlisted the help of a neighbor to ride into Kaycee and get a doctor to set Bill's leg, and for the only preacher, Phineas Phiben, to conduct a funeral. Bill was inconsolable. It seemed that his only reason for going on in life was to make a home for this beautiful girl and their child.

George and the neighbor dug a grave for Red Sky Woman and Elizabeth up on the hill northwest of the headquarters. When Phineas arrived with Bible in hand and discovered that the deceased was an Indian, he was indignant that he would have been asked to perform such a ceremony for a heathen.

A distraught Bill very quietly said, "That is all right preacher. She don't need none of your words. Her own God, Maheo, will protect her."

The preacher then admonished Bill for sinning in the sight of God by cohabiting with a heathen.

Bill's reply was, "My only sin was not being there for her."

Firing the Shanty   *Illustration by David Cook*

Tommy and Bill carefully placed rocks over the grave to protect Red Sky Woman and Elizabeth from the wolves and coyotes.

Bill moved into the small bunkhouse that had been used briefly by hired hands who could not accept the isolation or the work. He took all of his meals with the Thompsons and became part of their family.

Months later, George and Helen saw smoke rising from the direction of the other homestead. In his anguish, Bill had fired the cabin that he had shared with Red Sky Woman. No one questioned Bill about it and no one spoke of it again.

In the following years, Bill used the Thompson's horses to build dams all up and down Nine-Mile Wash to augment their meager earnings from the farm. During winter months he used the horses to freight supplies to the nearby Teapot Dome oilfield. Bill earned a good reputation for breaking horses that were then sold to the U.S. Cavalry during World War I.

As the years rolled by, both George and Helen were buried up on that hill overlooking the homestead, and their gravesites, along with those of Red Sky Woman and Elizabeth, were fenced in.

Tommy married and took over the farm. He and Ellie, his high school sweetheart, looked on Bill as a favorite uncle. He took his meals with them and he continued with the farm work and helped raise their children, "Sissie" and "Junior."

The whole countryside was being settled again and fences were being build everywhere. It was no longer necessary to control their enlarged cattle herd on the open range, and the aging Bill was still able to help and earn his keep.

In the early 1930s, Tommy deemed that their expanding farming operation would be better served by tractor power. The draft horses were sold, much to Bill's chagrin. He resented the smoke-belching behemoth whose irregular firing cadence marred the serenity of each spring and summer day, from dawn to sundown. He refused to have anything to do with it.

The barn became Bill's exclusive domain. It was immaculate. The tach room was as clean as most kitchens. The box stalls for the saddle horses remained in use during inclement weather. The wide stalls that had sheltered the work horses stood empty. But the four sets of harness, including collars and pads, were still hung on pegs with care. On rainy days, partly out of habit and partly out of respect, Bill would painstakingly wipe a thin coat of neatsfoot oil on every bit of exposed leather. It was as though his wishes and efforts might one day be rewarded by the return of the "gentle giant" Belgian draft horses. He yearned for a return to more gratifying days.

The saddle horses and cattle became Bill's sole responsibility. When Tommy once asked Bill about his need for four saddle horses, his reply was pretty simple: "I like to know that when I come in on a tired saddle horse, I'll have a fresh one ready to go." Bill was in his late sixties!

Freighting Supplies to Teapot Dome   *Illustration by David Cook*

CHAPTER 10

Late one afternoon, when Bill rode in to the ranch headquarters, he spotted a new 1941 model Ford automobile parked near the corral and a man in a business suit leaning on the corral fence.

Tom motioned for Bill to come over to the ranch house.

As Bill alighted from his tired saddle horse, he didn't just drop the reins as was his custom. He glanced warily at the stranger and then looked inquiringly at Tom.

"Bill, that fellow down there has come out here to talk to you," Tom said, and after a long pause, added, "Bill, he ain't armed."

Leading his saddle horse, Bill moved slowly toward the corral. His aging, aching bones gave mute testament to his seventy years and his rough life in the saddle.

As he approached, the stranger stuck out his hand and said, "Bill, I've come to see you on behalf of your brother, Ed."

"It's too bad, but you have wasted your time, mister, 'cause I ain't got a brother, let alone a brother named Ed."

"Okay, Elton Ellsworth Martin!"

Hearing his true name uttered for the first time in fifty years stunned Bill. His knees nearly gave away under him, and he had to grab onto a fence rail for support.

"I've been trailing you now for nearly a year, all over this God-forsaken part of Wyoming. If you will be so good as to show me that you ain't got a long white scar on your right forearm then I'll say, 'Sorry about the mistake,' and be on my way."

Bill fought through the maze of confusion that churned around in his brain. After a long silence, during which the stranger never lost eye contact with him, Bill heaved a sigh and said, "Let me unsaddle my horse and turn him out. Then we can visit over there on the porch of the bunkhouse."

It took Bill a long time to complete those chores as he debated with himself — "Can I run? At least he ain't a lawman. Why? Oh why now?"

Sensing that he could not put off the confrontation forever, after he had unsaddled, Bill hung his saddle from a rope in the tack room and carefully laid the saddle blanket out to dry. After he removed the bridle he watched his saddle horse roll in the dust, first on his right side a couple of times and then with a great heave roll completely over and then roll a couple of more times on his left side. He then got to his feet and shook himself violently to shake off some of the dust and then trotted out to the pasture.

Bill took his place in a chair on the bunkhouse porch, removed his hat and wiped his brow with a bandana and then asked,"Just supposin' that I am that guy you spoke of. What would you want of me?"

"Your brother Ed is getting along in years, just as you are, Bill", the stranger replied. "He has accumulated a lot of productive land back in Kansas and has become a very successful cow man. And, Elton, he truly does love you and has worried about you all of these years. He hired me to try to find you, and that sure as Hell ain't been easy."

There was a long uneasy pause.

"You ought to know that there ain't no warrants out for you over them killings up in Big Horn."

Bill sat a long time, non-committal, just letting that news settle in. Finally he looked over to where Tom was sitting. Tom had never taken his eyes off the two of them.

"And what else?" Bill queried.

"Ed wants you to come back to Kansas with me for a visit. And here is a return bus ticket that you are free to use at anytime. But knowing Ed as the fine man that he is, let me urge you to go back there with me and see him. He also wants you to know that your Mom has been dead for more than thirty years. That she missed you every day of her life after you had left. Ed thought you might want to visit her grave."

At the mention of Ma, Bill's eyes filled with tears for the first time since he had finished laying rocks over the graves of Red Sky Woman and their baby, Elizabeth.

Much later a very subdued Bill walked slowly over to the ranch house.

Tom, noting the distress in Bills demeanor, asked, "Bill, is everything all right? Is there anything I can do for you?"

"No, Tom, but I need to take a couple of weeks off to go visit my family. I'm sorry that I told you that I didn't have no family. I even lied when I talked about growing up in Texas. I even lied to you about my name."

That was something that Tom and his father before him had long suspected.

"Things are kinda slack around here right now, and I really do need to go visit."

"Bill, you know that you have always been your own man, and of course you are always free to go. And know that you will always have a place back here with me and Mom and the kids. We are your family, too!"

"Thanks", said Bill, and he trudged off to the bunkhouse to gather a few things for the trip. The stranger had waited patiently in the shade of the bunkhouse porch.

A month later, there was no mistaking the gait of the man that got out of the passenger side of the car that had just driven in and headed for the ranch house. But nothing else matched the old bronc rider. Not the felt hat, nor the white shirt, nor the Sunday-best trousers. Certainly not the high-top lace-up shoes, or the fresh haircut or the clean shave.

Nothing. Bill looked almost like a stranger to Tom and the family until he broke into an embarrassed grin and a "Good afternoon to yee."

Tom and the entire family were so glad to see him again that they eagerly asked questions, all at the same time.

Finally Bill held up his hand and said, "Whoa! Give me a chance!"

"Tom, it's hard for me to say this, but I have decided to go back to Kansas. I sure hope it won't put you in no bind. I'll always be appreciative of your Dad George, and then you, takin' me in all of these years."

"Bill, take your time and tell us all about it."

"I've decided to go back and be with my brother. I'll have my own house with electricity and running water and indoor plumbing, and I won't even have to cut wood 'cause the stove don't even need wood."

"I won't be doin' any more ropin' cause they have pens in each of the pastures to work the cattle in. All I have to do is count the cattle and check the windmills and keep the salt boxes filled. They don't run cattle during the winter to be looked after. So, I guess that during the winter, I'll just sit by the fireplace, exceptin' there ain't no fireplace."

"Well, Bill, how far will you be from town? Won't you need to learn to drive a car?"

"I tried that, and I ran Ed's new Ford into a pole. I don't want to try that again!"

"I'll just take my saddle and some of my clothes. The bedding and the clothes that I don't get packed, you can give to the fellow that takes my place."

"Here's my pistol. I wont be a needin' it back there, and you can give it to Junior when he is fifteen or sixteen years old or so. And, Sissie, will you put some wildflowers on Woman's grave whenever you are up thataway? I promise to write you some letters if you promise to answer them."

Then Bill trudged up the hill to the gravesites of Red Sky Woman and Elizabeth, as he had done so often through the years. Speaking out loud to himself and to the wind he said,"Well, I guess this is the last time we get to visit for a while."

"I'm sorry that I wasn't there, and that you had to die all alone."

"I am sorry that I never got around to putting up a marker with your names on it."

"I wish you had been here with me all of these years, and I wish you were going with me now."

"I am sorry that I never got around to telling you how important you were to me. I guess I didn't even know it at the time."

"Well, goodbye, and take care of yourself. I really did love you. I still do. And I always will."

The next morning a silence settled over the family as they sat around the breakfast table listening for the car to drive off. They all wondered if they would ever see Bill again.

When they heard the car driving away, Junior and Sissie fell into each others arms, sobbing uncontrollably. Tom and Ellie avoided looking at one another, not wanting to share their anguish.

Then, to their astonishment, they heard the familiar footsteps on the porch, the stomping of boots, and the squeaky kitchen door swinging open!

In walked Bill, work clothes, worn out boots and all. He seated himself at his usual place at the table as they all looked on in disbelief. Ellie immediately set a plate and silverware and a steaming cup of coffee in front of him.

"What happened, Bill? Why aren't you going back to the easy life with your family and all of that?"

Bill looked at his plate. Not at them.

Finally he said, "I had even put my saddle in the trunk of that car and had climbed into the front seat but for some reason I just couldn't close the door. They were being awfully nice to me back there, but they were trying to make me over into their own mold, and I kinda like me like I am.

Bill and Sissie Pick Wildflowers *Illustration by David Cook*

After just sittin' there for what must have been fifteen minutes, I just got back out of the car, slammed the door and took my saddle back out of the trunk. I thanked the fellow that had been a driving me and told him to be on his way. I finally realized that they really didn't need me back there. That you had become my true family. And you sure as Heck do need me!" It was the longest talk they had ever heard from Bill.

After a hearty breakfast, Junior retrieved Bill's pistol from the dresser drawer and handed it to Bill who promptly handed it back to him.

Sissie walked up the hill with Bill and they picked wildflowers along the way.

All was well with the world.